Charles Stewart Parnell
Uncrowned King of Ireland

Written by Rod Smith
and illustrated by Derry Dillon

IRELAND'S BEST KNOWN STORIES
IN A NUTSHELL
Heroes

Published 2017
Poolbeg Press Ltd

123 Grange Hill, Baldoyle
Dublin 13, Ireland

Text © Poolbeg Press Ltd 2017

A catalogue record for this book is available from the British Library.

ISBN 978 1 78199 859 5

Cover design and illustrations by Derry Dillon
Printed by GPS Colour Graphics Ltd, Alexander Road, Belfast BT6 9HP

To Betty and Jenny

SCOTLAND

IRELAND

MAYO
ROSCOMMON
Creggs
GALWAY
MEATH
DUBLIN
Glasnevin
Phoenix Park
O'Connell Street
Kilmainham
Cabinteely
WICKLOW
Avondale
ATLANTIC
OCEAN
CLARE
Ennis
IRISH SEA

ENGLAND

Manchester
DERBYSHIRE
Kirk Langley

Cambridge

WALES

LONDON ·Westminister

SOMERSET

Hove ·Brighton

A Wild Child

The year was 1852. A six-year-old Charles Stewart Parnell was running through the family estate at Avondale, in County Wicklow.

"*Slow down, Charles, or you'll fall!*" his mother Delia shouted.

"*I'll do what I want!*" he shouted and ran off into the distance.

"Master Charley is born to rule," said his nanny, Nurse Twopenny, and of course she was right.

Charles' father, John Henry Parnell, was a wealthy Anglo-Irish landowner. The Anglo-Irish were upper-class Irish people whose ancestors were English.

Charles' mother, Delia Tudor Stewart, was American. She was the daughter of an American naval hero, Admiral Charles Stewart, and Charles was named after him. Charles had five brothers and six sisters.

Charles' mother was very political and she hated the fact that the English were ruling Ireland from their Parliament in Westminster, London, and refusing to give the Irish "Home Rule" to govern themselves. She was so strong in her views that in the end her husband lost patience and forbade any political discussions at Avondale. Charles probably got his fiery spirit and interest in politics from her.

When Charles was still only six, his parents separated and he was sent off to a boarding school in Somerset, England. It was a girls' school, however, which he really resented! He was then sent to a boys' school at Kirk Langley in Derbyshire but he had to leave after he challenged the headmaster to a fight!

Back home, private teachers were arranged for him and his older brother John. Then he was sent to other schools in England. He was very difficult to teach and quarrelled with his teachers all the time. He had a big row with one teacher and had to apologise or be expelled. From this we can judge that he had a *very* strong personality!

When he finished school he went to Cambridge University, but left without finishing his course in 1869. While he was there he didn't like the way some English people treated the Irish.

"These English despise us because we are Irish. We must stand up to them," he told John.

Charles had inherited Avondale when his father died in 1859, after playing a cricket match while feeling unwell. So, when he left college he took over the day-to-day running of the estate. He was known as an "improving landlord" who got on well with his tenants – that is, the people who paid rent to live in houses or farm land on his estate.

Politics

In 1875 Charles was elected Home Rule Member of Parliament for County Meath. The party was led by Isaac Butt.

At that time there was an organisation called the "Fenians" which believed Ireland could only free itself from Britain through violent means. In 1876, Charles was accused of supporting "The Manchester Martyrs". These were three Fenians who were hanged for killing a policeman in Manchester in 1867 when they attacked a horse-drawn police van to free two of their leaders who had been arrested. While they were trying to blow the lock open, a policeman inside the van was shot. Charles and many other Irish people believed the policeman had been killed accidentally.

Around this time, Charles became friendly with some members of the Home Rule party who were known as "obstructionists". They were called this because their method was to "obstruct" or block the business of parliament. They made long boring speeches in the House of Commons to slow down the government as they wanted it to focus on Irish issues. "If we are not strong enough to get our own work done, we can stop them doing theirs," they said. Charles supported them and people began to consider him the leader of the party, and not Isaac Butt, the real leader.

In 1878, Charles agreed to help Michael Davitt in his work for tenants who were having trouble paying their rents to landlords, and were getting thrown out of their homes. Charles became President of the Irish National Land League. He attended huge public meetings throughout the country and urged tenants to "keep a firm grip on your homesteads and lands".

Michael Davitt was full of praise for Charles: "No man enjoying such growing popularity could be more modest, agreeable and charming . . . His laugh was most infectious."

Charles became so popular with the Irish people that a friend, a journalist called Tim Healy, called him "the uncrowned King of Ireland who paved the way for Ireland to take her place amongst the nations of the earth".

A Lady with a Rose

In the 1880 general election the Home Rule party won 63 seats. One of the new politicians elected was a Dublin man called Captain William O'Shea. Charles was invited to some dinner parties in a hotel in London by O'Shea but he never went.

O'Shea's wife Katharine came from quite an important family. She was the daughter of Sir John Page Wood, a baronet, and granddaughter of a former Lord Mayor of London. She and O'Shea had three children but the marriage was not a happy one, and by this time they were living apart. She later accused him of assaulting her, gambling on horses with her money, and meeting other women even though he was already married. However, to keep up appearances, she often was the hostess at dinner parties he held.

So one day Katharine took a cab to the House of Commons to invite Charles to dinner personally. Charles came out to meet her, and immediately she thought: 'This man is wonderful – and different.' He accepted her invitation and, when she leant forward in the cab to say goodbye, a rose she was wearing on her dress fell onto her skirt. Charles picked it up and placed it in his buttonhole.

It was love at first sight and the beginning of a relationship that was to have a huge impact on Irish politics for years to come.

Resisting the Landlords

In that same year, the Home Rule party helped to
persuade the British government, led by Prime Minister
William Gladstone and his Liberal party, to introduce
a law that would help tenants who had been forced
to leave their homes. It was hoped this would help to
stop violent protests and attacks against landlords in
Ireland.

At a meeting in Ennis in September 1880, Charles told the people to resist but not violently: "When a man takes a farm from another … shun him … to show your detestation of the crime he has committed." This policy of shunning or ignoring a person was called "boycotting" after Captain Charles Boycott who refused to reduce rents for tenants in Mayo and was shunned. He was eventually forced to leave the country.

When Michael Davitt was arrested in February 1881, Parnell and other MPs protested by blocking Gladstone from speaking in the House of Commons. They were forced to leave.

Gladstone introduced more laws in April 1881 to help tenants keep their homes and pay fair rents. Parnell made a speech against this as he thought the new laws did not give the tenants enough protection against greedy landlords. For this, he was arrested and sent to Kilmainham Gaol. Then the Land League encouraged the tenants to stop paying rent to bad landlords and it was declared an illegal organisation. The leaders were arrested but the Ladies' Land League, led by Charles' sister Anna, continued to help the tenants while the leaders were in prison.

Parnell was released from gaol on the 2nd of May 1882, after what some called "The Kilmainham Treaty" was agreed. Tenants agreed to start paying their rents again, if they were fair. Crimes against landlords were to be stopped.

Just four days later in the Phoenix Park, on the 6th of May, the murder took place of Frederick Cavendish, Chief Secretary for Ireland, and Under-Secretary Thomas Burke. They had been killed by a group of extreme Fenians known as "The Invincibles".

Charles and Michael Davitt were shocked and spoke out against the killings.

Punch magazine published a cartoon showing Charles and a monstrous figure. They called the Fenian movement "Frankenstein's Monster" and accused Charles of being like the character in the book *Frankenstein*, responsible for the creation of this monster. Charles was so upset that he offered to resign as a Member of Parliament. Gladstone persuaded him to remain.

After that, more Irish people began to support the Home Rule movement and turned their backs on acts of violence.

The Man Everybody Wants to See

Charles soon took complete control of the Home Rule Party. He changed its name to the Irish Parliamentary Party and he chose the candidates to run in elections. These people had to declare their support for him and promise to vote with the Party when the majority were in favour of a decision. His power and influence grew so much that in September 1883 *The United Irishman* newspaper wrote: **"Next to Gladstone, Parnell is the man everybody wants to see … he is an enormous present power."**

In January 1885, at a meeting in Cork, Charles spoke to the people about Home Rule: "No man has the right to fix the boundary of a nation … and say 'thus far shalt thou go and no further'."

In the 1885 general election, the Irish Parliamentary Party won 86 seats, which gave them a lot of power and influence in the House of Commons. Up until now there had been only two major political parties there: the Conservatives and the Liberals.

Captain O'Shea was not a popular politician, as people thought he was more interested in helping himself than helping others, but he won an election in Galway after getting strong support from Charles. People didn't know, however, that Charles was now living with O'Shea's wife Katharine. Katharine never set foot in Ireland so Charles spent a lot of his time living in England to be near the House of Commons and his family. He and Katharine had three children but the first, Claude Sophie, died in 1882 when only a few months old. Their second child Clare was born in 1883 and their third, Katie, was born in 1884. Katharine's daughter Norah also lived with them, while her other two children, Gerard and Carmen, stayed with the Captain.

Charles worked closely with the Liberal party to create a Home Rule Bill for Ireland in 1886. This act of parliament would allow Ireland to rule itself in most areas without interference from Britain. However, this was opposed by other politicians and the bill was defeated.

Then in 1887 some letters appeared in the *Times* newspaper, suggesting that Charles supported the Cavendish and Burke murders in the Phoenix Park in 1882. They turned out to be forgeries, created by a journalist called Richard Pigott. Charles sued the *Times* and was awarded £5,000 in damages. Now, with his good name restored, he returned to the House of Commons where politicians applauded when he rose to speak.

Gladstone continued to discuss the possibility of Home Rule for Ireland with Charles.

"Parnell is certainly one of the very best people to deal with that I have ever known," he said.

The Scandal

While these discussions were still taking place, Captain O'Shea filed for divorce on Christmas Eve, 1889. He accused his wife of being in a relationship with Charles. However, Captain O'Shea had always known about this. He had turned a blind eye to the situation as he was hoping Katharine's wealthy aunt, Aunt Ben, would leave money to him in her will. But Aunt Ben left all of her money to Katharine. Katharine's family were angry that they had been left nothing, so Captain O'Shea joined with them to contest the will. While this was going on, nobody was able to get to the money, not even Katharine, which was why O'Shea went to the divorce court.

He needed money and hoped that Charles and Katharine might agree to pay him off. They, however, didn't have enough money to do that. (In the end, some years after, Katharine had to settle for a much smaller amount than she was left by Aunt Ben – and she lost most of this money after giving it to a dishonest businessman to invest.)

Michael Davitt was worried about how a divorce case would affect Charles and the Home Rule movement. "Don't worry," Charles reassured him. "I will emerge without a stain on my name or reputation." Davitt thought this meant that O'Shea was lying about Charles and Katharine.

Charles did not oppose the divorce case in court because he was in love with Katharine and wanted to marry her. As they were not there to defend themselves, the court blamed Charles and Katharine for the break-up of the marriage. Captain O'Shea was granted the divorce in 1890 and was awarded the care of Charles' children, Clare and Katie. Charles and Katharine were deeply upset about this. They thought about running away to another country in Europe with the children, but this was not possible. O'Shea took the children away. However, they were returned to their mother two years later.

Meanwhile, Michael Davitt was very annoyed. He felt Charles had lied to him about his relationship to Katharine.

The Catholic Church was shocked. It did not believe in divorce. Archbishop Walsh of Dublin warned that Charles could not continue to be the leader of the Irish Parliamentary Party. Priests were encouraged to condemn Charles.

Even Gladstone sent a letter, warning that Charles could not continue as leader.

Others wanted him to step down for a while until the controversy blew over.

Charles refused.

"This is all a storm in a teacup," he said when he met Chief Secretary Morley of the British government.

"Mr Parnell, you might know Ireland, but you do not half know England," Mr. Morley replied.

On 1st December 1890, the Irish Parliamentary Party met at Committee Room 15 in the House of Commons to discuss Parnell's leadership.

"If we are to sell our leader, what are we getting for the price we are paying?" John Redmond asked. He was one of the younger members of the Irish Parliamentary Party, and a strong supporter of Charles.

"Don't sell me for nothing," Charles replied. "If you get my value you may change me tomorrow!"

"He must step down!" an angry Tim Healy demanded.

"Parnell is the master of the party," John Redmond declared.

"*Who is to be the mistress of the party?*" Tim Healy hissed.

This was an obvious insult to Katharine.

Charles became very angry. *"You are a cowardly little scoundrel who dares insult a woman!"* he roared.

Gone were the days when Tim Healy praised Charles as the "uncrowned King of Ireland".

After all the arguments, the party split into two groups. A group of 44, who were against Charles, left the room. Just 28 remained. The party remained divided for the next ten years.

Meanwhile, Charles married Katharine.

Failing Powers

Then, as he still had a lot of support in Ireland, Charles decided to tour the country to talk to the people. However, his health was not good.

He went to Kilkenny to support a candidate in an election and, as he was leaving a meeting, a mixture of mud, stones and slaked lime (a white powder that burns the skin) was thrown in his eyes. He recovered after a few days, but his health continued to suffer and became a serious concern to his friends.

Charles' choice of candidate in Kilkenny had a chance of winning the election. But the local priests visited the polling booths on the day of the election to prevent people from voting for him. Not surprisingly, Charles' candidate lost.

However, Charles refused to give up.

"I will contest every election in the country," he said. "I will fight while I live!"

At a public meeting in Cabinteely, County Dublin, he got wet when he spoke to the people in the pouring rain. He met his sister Emily for dinner afterwards and sat in his wet clothes during the meal. This did not help his health, which continued to get worse. He was suffering from rheumatism and kidney disease but he refused to see a doctor.

Katharine tried to persuade him to get some help. "Come away with me, my King," she said, using her pet name for him. "You need to get away from this struggle and get some rest."

"Queenie," he said, "I would rather die now than give in, but if you say it, I will do it."

But Katharine would not force him to give up as she knew how important this was to him.

When he finally agreed to see Dr Kenny in Dublin, he was told not to go to any more public meetings until his health improved.

"Nonsense, Dr Kenny!" said Charles. "I have made a promise and I will not disappoint my audience."

He made his way to the village of Creggs which is on the border of Galway and Roscommon. It was his last ever public meeting. Even though his arm was in a sling because of his rheumatism and he was in pain, he remained defiant when he began to speak.

"We shall continue this fight … for freedom … I will not leave until they get a better leader!"

The rain fell as he spoke, and he got wet again. After the meeting, he had to sit in wet clothes once again.

Katharine had gone to their rented house at Walsingham Terrace, in Hove, near Brighton in England. Charles left Ireland and joined her there.

When he arrived, on Thursday, 1st October 1891, she immediately knew that he was very sick.

She lit a fire as Charles felt very cold. They had a meal together. She then helped him up the stairs to bed, as he was too weak to walk up on his own.

Over the next day or two Charles began to feel a little better. However, by Monday, he was in a lot of pain and had a high fever. He spent most of Tuesday sleeping lightly.

That evening he woke up briefly and spoke to Katharine.

"Kiss me, sweet wifie, and I will try to sleep a little."

She lay beside him and kissed him. He died in her arms that night, the 6th of October 1891, at the very early age of 45.

When his body was placed in the coffin, Katharine dropped a withered rose beside him before the lid was closed. It was the same rose Charles had taken from her the very first time they met.

Farewell to Parnell

Over 200,000 people lined the streets of Dublin to pay their respects as the funeral cortège passed by. Charles' favourite horse, Home Rule, walked behind the hearse, carrying a pair of boots and stirrups that Charles once wore. It took over four hours to reach Charles' final resting place at Glasnevin Cemetery because of the crowds.

Years later a gravestone was placed to mark his final resting place. It is a large block of Wicklow granite with one word: PARNELL. Such is his fame, no more needs to be said.

The split in the Irish Parliamentary Party was finally healed in 1900 under the leadership of John Redmond. Ireland would have to wait until 1912 for the next chance of Home Rule. But this never came to pass because of the outbreak of World War I and the Easter Rising in 1916.

In 1911 the Parnell Monument was erected on O'Connell Street, Dublin, where it can still be seen today, and Parnell's Avondale estate is now owned by the state and is open to the public, so you can go visit it.

The Sunday nearest to the 6th of October (the day he died) is called *Ivy Day* in Parnell's memory. A wreath of ivy was sent by a Cork woman to his funeral "as the best offering she could afford". Seeing this, the mourners took ivy leaves from the walls and stuck them in their coat lapels. Ever after, the ivy leaf became the emblem for Parnell's followers.

Parnell is hugely important in Irish history. The famous historian F.S.L. Lyons said that he gave the Irish people back their self-respect.

The great poet William Butler Yeats wrote poems about Parnell. One of them, called *"Come Gather Round Me, Parnellites"*, talks about the two great loves in his life – his country and Katharine:

"He fought the might of England
And saved the Irish poor,
Whatever good a farmer's got
He brought it all to pass . . .
Every man that sings a song
Keeps Parnell in his mind . . .
For Parnell was a proud man
No prouder trod the ground . . .
And Parnell loved his country
And Parnell loved his lass."

The End

GLOSSARY (alphabetical order)

agent: a person who does business for another person

assaulting: attacking

baronet: a title of honour in Britain for a person who is not of noble birth; it is a lower rank than baron

bill: a proposed law, one that has not yet been passed into law

booths: enclosed compartments that allow privacy, for example when telephoning, voting, or sitting in a restaurant

boundary: a line which marks the limit of an area

candidates: people seeking to be elected to office

contest: compete for something or oppose something

cortège: a procession at a serious event

controversy: a lot of disagreement or argument about something

defiant: boldly resistant or challenging

despise: to dislike someone because you think they have no value

detestation: hatred

divorce: a legal end to a marriage

elected: chosen to hold public office or some other position by voting

emblem: a design or picture of something that stands for a group or an idea

erected: to set something up, for example a building or wall

estate: land in the country, usually with a large house, owned by one family

extreme: the highest degree or farthest point; extreme beliefs are unreasonable ones

filed: submitted a legal document or application, to be placed on record

forbade: commanded someone not to do something

forgeries: fake documents, signatures, banknotes, or work of art

F.S.L. Lyons: Francis Stewart Leland Lyons, a famous historian who was Provost at Trinity College, Dublin. He was the author of an excellent biography of Parnell

***Frankenstein*:** a novel written by Mary Shelley in 1818 about a scientist, Victor Frankenstein, who builds a human-like creature with human feelings and emotions

gambling: betting money on something

Gladstone: William Ewart Gladstone, leader of the British Liberal party, and British Prime Minister at four different times during the late 1800s

govern: rule

granite: a hard rock

homestead: a house, especially a farmhouse

House of Commons: the British house of parliament whose members are elected by the public

illegal: against the law

impact: a strong effect

infectious: easily spread from one to another

influence: power to affect people

inherited: received something from someone in their will after their death

interference: unwanted involvement in the activities of others

invest: put money into some scheme which promises to increase your money

invincible: cannot be defeated

journalist: a person who writes for newspapers, magazines, or news websites

league: a collection of people, countries, or groups that combine for a common purpose

majority: the greater part or number; the number larger than half of the total

martyr: a person who is killed for their cause or religion

mayor: the head of a town, elected by council members; Lord Mayor is the title of the mayor in certain large cities

modest: humble, not boastful

monument: a statue or building erected in memory of a person or event

naval: connected to the navy

opposed: acted against; resisted to

organisation: a group of people who work together for a shared purpose

outbreak: a sudden violent occurrence

parliament: the group of people who are responsible for making the laws in a government

paved the way: made progress easier (like paving a road with stone, concrete or tar)

personality: how a person behaves and what they are like

political: about politics which is the activities associated with the governing of a country

polling: recording the votes of

reputation: what people think about you

reduce: make smaller

resented: bitterly disliked

resign: volunteer to leave a job or office

resist: refuse to accept or try to prevent

restored: brought back to its original condition

scandal: an action that damages your reputation

shalt: shall not

sue: try to get a court of law to make a person, company, or organization to pay because they have treated a person unfairly or hurt that person in some way

support: agree with or approve of

thou: you

thus: to this degree or extent

treaty: a signed agreement between countries

trod: walked (from 'to tread')

violent: with rough force

Some Things to Talk About

1. Where did Charles live?
2. What kind of a person was his mother?
3. Did Charles like school?
4. What kind of a landlord was Charles?
5. What county did Charles represent in the 1875 election?
6. What was Charles' view on "The Manchester Martyrs"?
7. What were "obstructionists"?
8. What help did Charles give to Michael Davitt?
9. Why was Charles called "the uncrowned King of Ireland"?
10. What happened to Captain Charles Boycott?
11. What was the "Kilmainham Treaty"?
12. How did Anna Parnell help her brother Charles?
13. What did the group known as "The Invincibles" do in May 1882?
14. Who was Richard Pigott?
15. Why do you think Captain O'Shea decided to divorce Katharine?
16. Was Charles able to continue as leader of the Irish Parliamentary Party after the divorce?
17. Where was Katharine when Charles died?
18. What followed after the hearse at Charles' funeral?
19. What did Katharine put into his coffin? Why did she?
20. Where is Charles buried? What marks his grave?
21. What is *Ivy Day*?

Timeline

1846: Parnell is born in Avondale, Co. Wicklow

1852: Is sent to a girls' boarding school in England and later to other schools there

1859: Inherits Avondale estate after the death of his father

1869: Leaves Cambridge University without finishing his course

1875: Is elected MP for Meath

1876: Declares support for "The Manchester Martyrs"

1878: Agrees to help Michael Davitt

1879: Becomes President of the Irish Land League

1880: Tells tenants to "boycott" people who take farms from other tenants
Home Rule Party wins 63 seats in the general election
Meets Katharine O'Shea

1881: Is arrested and sent to Kilmainham Gaol for not supporting Gladstone's Land Act

1882: Is released from Kilmainham Gaol
Cavendish and Burke murdered at Phoenix Park
Home Rule Party becomes Irish Parliamentary Party
Claude Sophie born, and dies a few months later

1883: His daughter Clare is born

1884: His daughter Katie is born

1885: Irish Parliamentary Party wins 86 seats in the general election (85 in Ireland and 1 in Liverpool)

1887: *The Times* publishes letters that supposedly link Charles to the Phoenix Park murders in 1882

1889: Richard Pigott admits he forged the letters that claimed Parnell was involved in the murders
Charles returns to the House of Commons and receives a standing ovation
Captain O'Shea files for divorce and wins the case, plus custody of Parnell's children

1890: Catholic Church and William Gladstone do not support Charles as leader of the Irish Parliamentary Party, which splits into two

1891: Charles marries Katharine
Charles's health begins to deteriorate after getting wet at public meetings in Cabinteely and Creggs
Charles dies at the age of 45 in Katharine's arms at their home in Hove, near Brighton

1900: Irish Parliamentary Party reunited under John Redmond

1911: Parnell monument erected in O'Connell Street, Dublin

1937: Hollywood releases a movie, *Parnell*, starring one of the most famous actors at the time, Clark Gable, as Parnell. Captain O'Shea's son, Gerard, has a role as a paid advisor to the makers of the movie. The movie was not a success and is included in the book *The Fifty Worst Films of All Time* by Harry Medved, with Randy Dreyfuss and Michael Medved. (It is still worth watching however!)

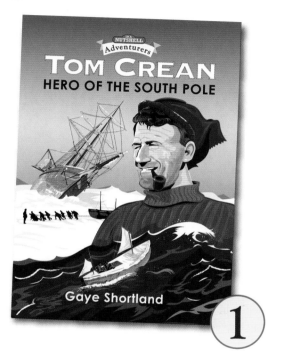

In 1918, sailors from the famous polar ship *Endurance* recorded a ballad about one of their fellow crew members. The chorus went:

Hail, hail, Tom Crean, hail, hail, Tom Crean,
He's the bravest man that the world's ever seen.
Hail, hail, Tom Crean, hail, hail, Tom Crean,
He's the Irish giant from County Kerry!

So who was this man hailed as a hero and loved and respected so much? Who "faced death many times and never backed down"? And how did this farmer's son from Kerry, who ran away to join the navy at 15, come to be such a famous Antarctic explorer? This is his amazing story.